123
For The Birds
PEANUTS

# Fooled You, BERT!

**by Jocelyn Stevenson · Illustrated by Bill Williams**

**Featuring Jim Henson's Sesame Street Muppets**

A SESAME STREET/GOLDEN PRESS BOOK
Published by Western Publishing Company, Inc.
in conjunction with Children's Television Workshop.


Library of Congress Catalog Number: 80-83289
ISBN 0-307-23128-3

One day Ernie decided to play a joke or two on his old buddy Bert. He found Bert sitting on the stoop, reading a book about birds. Bert had just come to the really good page about pigeons when Ernie interrupted.

"Pardon me, old buddy, but your shoe's untied."

"Oh, thanks, Ernie," said Bert. He leaned over to tie his shoe. But both of his saddle oxfords were neatly tied!

"Fooled you, Bert!" said Ernie.

"Very funny, Ernie," said Bert.

Bert found his page and started reading again.

"Hey, Bert!" said Ernie. "What's green and slimy, has five legs and a hairy face?"

"I don't know, Ernie," sighed Bert. "What's green and slimy, has five legs and a hairy face?"

"I don't know either, Bert, but it's crawling on your arm!"

"Yow!" yelled Bert. He jumped up and looked at his arm. There was absolutely nothing there.

"Khe-khe-khe," laughed Ernie. "Fooled you, Bert!"

"Hilarious joke, Ernie," said Bert. "I think I'll go inside and polish my paper clips. So leave me alone, okay?"

"Sure, Bert," said Ernie, and he followed Bert inside.

Bert took out his paper clips. "Nothing beats shiny paper clips," he said happily as he started to polish them. Pretty soon he heard Ernie walking into the bathroom.

Suddenly, Ernie yelled, “Bert! Bert! Come quick! The bathtub is overflowing!”

Bert leaped up, spilling paper clips all over the floor. “Oh no!” he said. He grabbed a mop. “I’m coming, Ernie!”

There was Ernie, standing by the sink playing with Rubber Duckie.

"Fooled you, Bert," he said.

"Ha. Ha. Ha," said Bert without smiling.

Bert turned to go, but Ernie grabbed his arm. "Wait, Bert!" he said. "Stick out your tongue."

Bert stuck out his tongue. Ernie gasped. "Oh no!"

"What, what, what?" said Bert.

Ernie covered his eyes. "Oh, Bert! You've got horrible green spots all over your tongue!"

"Help!" screamed Bert. He ran to the mirror, opened his mouth and stuck out his tongue. It was just as pink and perfect as could be.

"Ernie," said Bert slowly, "what's the big idea?"

"Fooled you, Bert," said Ernie.

"I'm going to count my bottlecaps now, Ernie," said Bert. "Please leave me alone."

"Okay, old buddy," said Ernie. "I'm going to the store."

Bert had just begun to count his Figgy Fizz bottlecaps when the phone rang. "Hello?" he said.

"Is Ernie there?" said the voice on the phone.

"No, Ernie's gone to the store. May I take a message?"

"Please tell him that Chris and the Alphabeats will be over at 3 o'clock for band practice."

"Now, just a minute!" said Bert.

"Oh...and one more thing," said the voice.

"What?" asked Bert.

"Fooled you, Bert!" It was Ernie, of course.

"Bert!" called Ernie, as he returned a few minutes later. "You won't believe what I just saw coming down Sesame Street."

"Right, Ernie, I don't believe it. I'm not going to listen to anything else you say today. Now I want to listen to my marching music record," said Bert. "No more jokes, okay?"

"Whatever you say, Bert," Ernie agreed. "But I've never seen anything so *huge*.

"Gee, imagine that. They're *plaid*, too!"

"Oh, come on, Ernie," said Bert. "I can't listen to my music when you keep interrupting."

“Wow. Look at those horns!” exclaimed Ernie.

Finally, Bert couldn't stand it anymore. He jumped up and ran over to the window. Of course, there was nothing unusual to see on Sesame Street.

"Where are the elephants, Ernie?" asked Bert.

"What elephants, Bert?"

"The plaid ones playing the horns!"

"Huh? Oh, you mean the huge, plaid things with horns? Fooled you, Bert!"

Now Bert was angry. "Listen, Ernie, how would you like it if you were trying to do something important, and someone kept fooling you? I'll tell you, Ernie. You wouldn't like it, and neither do I. So leave me alone. No more fooling, Ernie."

"Okay, Bert," Ernie sighed, "I'll go put the groceries away."

Bert settled down with his book again. It was peaceful and quiet in the apartment at last.

"Let's see," he thought. "Ernie has been playing tricks on me all day. He made me think my shoelaces were untied.

He told me there was a green slimy bug on my arm.

He said that the bathtub was overflowing.

He said there were horrible green spots on my tongue.

I thought his friends were coming over for rock and roll practice.

He made me think that a band of plaid elephants was marching down Sesame Street!

"I wonder what Ernie is up to now...."

It was quiet in the apartment, all right—too quiet.

Just as Bert was imagining what terrible tricks Ernie might be cooking up in the kitchen, Ernie came into the living room with a covered tray.

"I made a wonderful surprise for you, old buddy," said Ernie.

"Oh sure, Ernie," said Bert. "It's probably another one of your terrific jokes."

"No, Bert. This time it's something you'll really like," said Ernie. "Come on, Bert, just take a peek!"

"No, I'm not going to let you trick me again, Ernie," Bert answered. "It's probably something disgusting. I'm not going to look."

"Well, then, I'll show you, Bert!"

Ernie took the cover off the tray with a flourish. "Here! I made you some delicious oatmeal cookies. Your very favorites!"

Bert stared in surprise.

"This time you really fooled me, Ernie!"